Saxophone Sits Alone

Jay C. Peterson

To order additional copies of this book, contact:
Xlibris
844-714-8691
www.Xlibris.com
Orders@Xlibris.com

ISBN: Softcover   978-1-6641-5826-9
        EBook   978-1-6641-5825-2

Print information available on the last page

Rev. date: 03/10/2021

This book is dedicated to my brother Jed, and anyone else who has suffered the judgement of others for being different. May you continue to be yourself and inspire others to do the same.

This is a story about Saxophone. Saxophone loved making music and was trying to find someone to play with. The music room was filled with many different sounds.

She looked over at the woodwind instruments playing together and smiled. "I'll play with them." she decided.

When the woodwind instruments saw Saxophone, they turned their backs to her. Saxophone was confused. "Flute," she said, "may I play with you?"

Flute looked at the other woodwind instruments and then back at Saxophone. "We don't want to play with you."

"Why not?" Saxophone asked with a low voice.

"You look nothing like us." argued Oboe, pointing at Saxophone's bell. "Look! You're covered with brass!" The other woodwind instruments started to laugh.

Saxophone looked down at her body. "Why does that matter?" she turned to Clarinet and pointed to her reed, "Here, I have a reed, just like you."

"You don't sound like me," responded Clarinet, "you sound... different!" The woodwind instruments laughed some more. "Go play with someone else!"

As the woodwind instruments moved away from Saxophone, she noticed the brass instruments playing together on the other side of the room. When they saw Saxophone walking up to them, the brass instruments turned their backs to her. "Trombone," Saxophone said, "may I play with you?"

Trombone looked at the other brass instruments and then at Saxophone. "We don't want to play with you."

"Why not?" Saxophone asked with a low voice. "My body is brass, just like yours."

"You are nothing like us." argued Trumpet, pointing at Saxophone's reed. "Look! You don't even have a proper mouthpiece!"

"Why does that matter?" Saxophone showed them her bell. "Here, I have a bell, just like all of you."

"You don't sound like us," responded Tuba, "you sound... different!" The brass instruments laughed at Saxophone. "Go play with someone else!"

Saxophone had no one to play with. She felt very sad and very lonely. She went to the far corner of the music room. When she got there, Saxophone sat all alone. "Why am I so different?" she cried, "I wish I could change. I wish I could be someone else. Anything but a saxophone."

Just then, she heard a voice. "Why are you crying?" The voice was coming from above her. She looked up and saw Piano staring down at her.

"Why are you crying?" Piano asked again. "Nobody wants to play with me," Saxophone whimpered, "they don't like me because I'm different."

Piano nodded, "I know how you feel. Nobody wants to play with me either."

Saxophone sniffled, "Really? Why not?"

"I'm different too," Piano explained, "I wanted to play with the percussion instruments, but they didn't like me because I use strings to make my music."

"They laughed at me and told me to go play with someone else."

"So, I went to play with the string instruments, but they didn't like me either, because I don't look like them, or play like them. I use my keys to make sounds, instead of using a bow or a pick."

"That's why I'm here in this corner, because nobody wants me around."

Saxophone was shocked, "That's awful." She looked at her body, and then at Piano's body. "Would you like to play with me?"

Piano looked at Saxophone's body, and then at his body. "We are very different," he said.

"Why does that matter?" Saxophone asked.

"Hmm, maybe it doesn't." Piano agreed, "Alright Saxophone, I'll play with you."

Together, as a duet, Saxophone and Piano started to play. It was a sound that Saxophone had never heard before. It was… different. The different sounds from Piano and Saxophone came together to make something new.

All of the other instruments stopped when they heard Piano and Saxophone playing. It was a sound that none of them had ever heard before. When the performance was over, everyone cheered.

Piano looked down at Saxophone and smiled. "I understand now. It's good to be different. If everyone sounded the same, there would be no new music to discover. Thank you Saxophone! Thank you for letting me play with you."

Saxophone nodded, "You're welcome."

Just then, Flute walked up to Trombone. "Trombone," she asked, "Would you like to play with me?" "Sure," Trombone said. "I'll play with you."

Together, as a duet, Flute and Trombone started to play. It was a sound that none of them had ever heard before. It was… different. As they continued to play, other instruments began asking to play with someone different.

Soon, everyone was making new music, together. The violin was playing with the bassoon, the xylophone was playing with the cello, the tuba was playing with the oboe, the clarinet was playing with the guitar and the trumpet was playing with the drums.

Everyone found someone different to play with. The music room was filled with harmony. Saxophone looked around at all of the instruments. "We're all the same because we're all different. Each of us has something special and unique to share with the world. As long as we are willing to listen, there will always be new music to find."

She looked down at her body and smiled, "I will always be different, but I will never be alone."

Printed in the United States
by Baker & Taylor Publisher Services